# Nonsense Poems

## EDWARD LEAR

DOVER PUBLICATIONS, INC.
New York

# DOVER CHILDREN'S THRIFT CLASSICS
## EDITOR OF THIS VOLUME: CANDACE WARD

Published in Canada by General Publishing Company, Ltd., 30 Lesmill Road, Don Mills, Toronto, Ontario.

Published in the United Kingdom by Constable and Company, Ltd., 3 The Lanchesters, 162–164 Fulham Palace Road, London W6 9ER.

### Bibliographical Note

*Nonsense Poems* is a new collection of nonsense verse written and illustrated by Edward Lear, first published by Dover Publications, Inc. in 1994. These poems were originally published in *A Book of Nonsense* (1846), *Nonsense Songs, Stories, Botany, and Alphabets* (1871), *More Nonsense, Pictures, Rhymes, Botany, etc.* (1872), *Laughable Lyrics, A Fourth Book of Nonsense Poems, Songs, Botany, Music, etc.* (1877) and *Nonsense Songs and Stories* (1895).

### Library of Congress Cataloging-in-Publication Data

Lear, Edward, 1812–1888.
  Nonsense poems / Edward Lear.
      p.    cm. — (Dover children's thrift classics)
    Summary: A new collection of nonsense verses, many beginning "There was an old man . . ." or "There was a young lady . . ."
    ISBN 0-486-28031-4 (pbk.)
    1. Children's poetry, English.  2. Nonsense verses, English.
  [1. Nonsense verses.  2. English poetry.]  I. Title.  II. Series.
  PR4879.L2N59   1994
  821'.8—dc20                                                93-39193
                                                                CIP
                                                                 AC

Manufactured in the United States of America
Dover Publications, Inc., 31 East 2nd Street, Mineola, N.Y. 11501

# Note

EDWARD LEAR was born on May 12, 1812, the twentieth of twenty-one children. He was a strange-looking child, shortsighted and with a very large nose, who suffered from asthma, bronchitis and epilepsy. Perhaps his ill health contributed to his withdrawn character, but for whatever reason, Lear spent much of his childhood writing poetry, sketching and reading books on natural history.

In 1832 Lear was commissioned by Lord Stanley, later 13th Earl of Derby, to illustrate a book on his private menagerie of over 300 animals and 1700 birds. For the next five years, Lear lived with his patron's family, endearing himself to the household's many children with his nonsensical stories and songs. The result of these spontaneous entertainments was Lear's first *Book of Nonsense*, published anonymously in 1846. Although Lear was an accomplished artist, and at one time Queen Victoria's drawing master, today he is best remembered for his illustrated nonsense verse.

# Contents

iv

There was an Old Man of Dee-side,
Whose hat was exceedingly wide,
But he said "Do not fail, if it happen to hail
To come under my hat at Dee-side!"

There was an Old Man with a nose,
Who said, "If you choose to suppose,
That my nose is too long, you are certainly
    wrong!"
That remarkable Man with a nose.

1

There was an Old Man on a hill,
Who seldom, if ever, stood still;
He ran up and down, in his Grandmother's
   gown,
Which adorned that Old Man on a hill.

There was an Old Man at a casement,
Who held up his hands in amazement;
When they said, "Sir! you'll fall!" he replied,
   "Not at all!"
That incipient Old Man at a casement.

There was an Old Person of Burton,
Whose answers were rather uncertain;
When they said, "How d'ye do?" he replied,
    "Who are you?"
That distressing Old Person of Burton.

There was an Old Man of th' Abruzzi,
So blind that he couldn't his foot see;
When they said, "That's your toe," he replied,
    "Is it so?"
That doubtful Old Man of th' Abruzzi.

There was an Old Person of Ewell,
Who chiefly subsisted on gruel;
But to make it more nice, he inserted some
mice,
Which refreshed that Old Person of Ewell.

There was an Old Man of Aôsta,
Who possessed a large Cow, but he lost her;
But they said, "Don't you see, she has rushed
up a tree?
You invidious Old Man of Aôsta!"

There was a Young Lady of Poole,
Whose soup was excessively cool;
So she put it to boil by the aid of some oil,
That ingenious Young Lady of Poole.

There was an Old Man of Thames Ditton,
Who called for something to sit on;
But they brought him a hat, and said—"Sit
    upon that,
You abruptious old man of Thames Ditton."

There was an Old Man of Whitehaven,
Who danced a quadrille with a Raven;
But they said—"It's absurd, to encourage this
    bird!"
So they smashed that Old Man of Whitehaven.

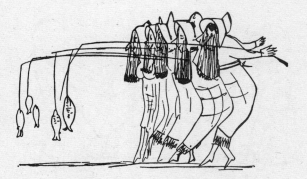

There was an Old Man of Marseilles,
Whose daughters wore bottle-green veils;
They caught several Fish, which they put in a
    dish,
And sent to their Pa' at Marseilles.

There was an Old Person of Slough,
Who danced at the end of a bough;
But they said, "If you sneeze, you might damage
the trees,
You imprudent Old Person of Slough."

There was an Old Person of Fife,
Who was greatly disgusted with life;
They sang him a ballad, and fed him on salad,
Which cured that Old Person of Fife.

There was an Old Person of Crowle,
Who lived in the nest of an owl;
When they screamed in the nest, he screamed
   out with the rest,
That depressing Old Person of Crowle.

There was an Old Person in gray,
Whose feelings were tinged with dismay;
She purchased two parrots, and fed them with
   carrots,
Which pleased that Old Person in gray.

There was a Young Lady of Greenwich,
Whose garments were border'd with Spinach;
But a large spotty Calf, bit her shawl quite in
half,
Which alarmed that Young Lady of Greenwich.

There was an Old Man in a tree,
Whose whiskers were lovely to see;
But the birds of the air, pluck'd them perfectly
bare,
To make themselves nests in that tree.

There was an Old Man of Melrose,
Who walked on the tips of his toes;
But they said, "It ain't pleasant, to see you at
    present,
You stupid Old Man of Melrose."

There was an Old Man with a beard,
Who said, "It is just as I feared!—
Two Owls and a Hen, four Larks and a Wren,
Have all built their nests in my beard!"

There was a Young Lady of Ryde,
Whose shoe-strings were seldom untied;
She purchased some clogs, and some small
  spotty dogs,
And frequently walked about Ryde.

There was an Old Person of Jodd,
Whose ways were perplexing and odd;
She purchased a whistle, and sate on a thistle.
And squeaked to the people of Jodd.

There was a Young Lady of Norway,
Who casually sat in a doorway;
When the door squeezed her flat, she exclaimed
    "What of that?"
This courageous Young Lady of Norway.

There was a Young Lady of Hull,
Who was chased by a virulent Bull;
But she seized on a spade, and called out—
    "Who's afraid!"
Which distracted that virulent Bull.

There was an Old Person of Rimini,
Who said, "Gracious! Goodness! O Gimini!"
When they said, "Please be still!" she ran down
    a hill,
And was never more heard of at Rimini.

There was an Old Person of Rye,
Who went up to town on a fly;
But they said, "If you cough, you are safe to fall
    off!
You abstemious Old Person of Rye!"

There was an Old Man, who when little
Fell casually into a kettle;
But, growing too stout, he could never get out,
So he passed all his life in that kettle.

There was an Old Man at a Junction,
Whose feelings were wrung with compunction,
When they said "The Train's gone!" he ex-
    claimed "How forlorn!"
But remained on the rails of the Junction.

There was an Old Man, on whose nose
Most birds of the air could repose;
But they all flew away, at the closing of day,
Which relieved that Old Man and his nose.

There was an Old Person of Bray,
Who sang through the whole of the day
To his ducks and his pigs, whom he fed upon
    figs,
That valuable Person of Bray.

There is a Young Lady, whose nose
Continually prospers and grows;
When it grew out of sight, she exclaimed in a
    fright,
"Oh! Farewell to the end of my nose!"

There was an Old Man of Messina,
Whose daughter was named Opsibeena;
She wore a small wig, and rode out on a pig,
To the perfect delight of Messina.

There was an Old Man who said, "How
Shall I flee from this horrible Cow?
I will sit on this stile, and continue to smile,
Which may soften the heart of that Cow."

There was an Old Man in a pew,
Whose waistcoat was spotted with blue;
But he tore it in pieces, to give to his nieces,—
That cheerful Old Man in a pew.

There was a Young Person of Bantry,
Who frequently slept in the pantry;
When disturbed by the mice, she appeased
    them with rice,
That judicious Young Person of Bantry.

There was an Old Person of Basing,
Whose presence of mind was amazing;
He purchased a steed, which he rode at full
    speed,
And escaped from the people of Basing.

There was an Old Lady of Prague,
Whose language was horribly vague.
When they said, "Are these caps?" she an-
    swered, "Perhaps!"
That oracular Lady of Prague.

There was an Old Person of Sparta,
Who had twenty-five sons and one daughter;
He fed them on snails, and weighed them in
    scales,
That wonderful Person of Sparta.

There was an Old Person of Dover,
Who rushed through a field of blue Clover;
But some very large bees, stung his nose and
  his knees,
So he very soon went back to Dover.

There was an Old Person of Anerley,
Whose conduct was strange and unmannerly;
He rushed down the Strand, with a Pig in each
  hand,
But returned in the evening to Anerley.

There was an Old Man of Dundee,
Who frequented the top of a tree;
When disturbed by the crows, he abruptly arose,
And exclaimed, "I'll return to Dundee."

There was an Old Man of the North,
Who fell into a basin of broth;
But a laudable cook, fished him out with a
  hook,
Which saved that Old Man of the North.

There was an Old Person of Prague,
Who was suddenly seized with the plague;
But they gave him some butter, which caused
     him to mutter,
And cured that Old Person of Prague.

There was an Old Man of Apulia,
Whose conduct was very peculiar;
He fed twenty sons, upon nothing but buns,
That whimsical Man of Apulia.

There was an Old Person of Chili,
Whose conduct was painful and silly;
He sate on the stairs, eating apples and pears,
That imprudent Old Person of Chili.

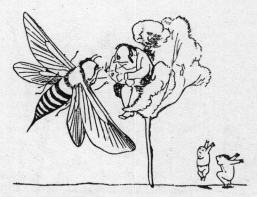

There was an Old Man in a tree,
Who was horribly bored by a Bee;
When they said, "Does it buzz?" he replied,
    "Yes, it does!
It's a regular brute of a Bee!"

There was an Old Lady of Chertsey,
Who made a remarkable curtsey;
She twirled round and round, till she sunk
    underground,
Which distressed all the people of Chertsey.

There was a Young Lady of Lucca,
Whose lovers completely forsook her;
She ran up a tree, and said, "Fiddle-de-dee!"
Which embarrassed the people of Lucca.

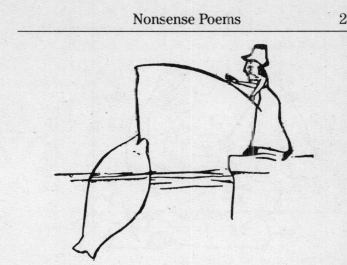

There was a Young Lady of Wales,
Who caught a large fish without scales;
When she lifted her hook, she exclaimed, "Only
look!"
That ecstatic Young Lady of Wales.

There was an Old Man in a boat,
Who said, "I'm afloat! I'm afloat!"
When they said, "No! you ain't!" he was ready
to faint,
That unhappy Old Man in a boat.

There was an Old Person of Ickley,
Who could not abide to ride quickly;
He rode to Karnak, on a tortoise's back,
That moony Old Person of Ickley.

There was an Old Man of the West,
Who never could get any rest;
So they set him to spin, on his nose and his
    chin,
Which cured that Old Man of the West.

There was an Old Person of Woking,
Whose mind was perverse and provoking;
He sate on a rail, with his head in a pail,
That illusive Old Person of Woking.

There was an Old Lady of France,
Who taught little ducklings to dance;
When she said, "Tick-a-tack!"—They only said,
    "Quack!"
Which grieved that Old Lady of France.

There was an Old Person of Gretna,
Who rushed down the crater of Etna;
When they said, "Is it hot?" he replied, "No, it's
    not!"
That mendacious Old Person of Gretna.

There was an Old Person of Bree,
Who frequented the depths of the sea;
She nurs'd the small fishes, and washed all the
    dishes,
And swam back again into Bree.

There was an Old Man of Toulouse,
Who purchased a new pair of shoes;
When they asked, "Are they pleasant?"—He
    said, "Not at present!"
That turbid Old Man of Toulouse.

There was a Young Girl of Majorca,
Whose aunt was a very fast walker;
She walked seventy miles, and leaped fifteen
    stiles,
Which astonished that Girl of Majorca.

There was a Young Lady whose nose
Was so long that it reached to her toes;
So she hired an Old Lady, whose conduct was
    steady,
To carry that wonderful nose.

There was an Old Man in a Marsh,
Whose manners were futile and harsh;
He sate on a log, and sang songs to a frog,
That instructive Old Man in a Marsh.

There was an Old Person of Brill,
Who purchased a shirt with a frill;
But they said, "Don't you wish, you may'nt look
   like a fish,
You obsequious Old Person of Brill?"

There was an Old Person of Wick,
Who said, "Tick-a-Tick, Tick-a-Tick;
Chickabee, Chickabaw," and he said nothing
   more,
That laconic Old Person of Wick.

There was an Old Man with a beard,
Who sat on a horse when he reared;
But they said, "Never mind! you will fall off
    behind,
You propitious Old Man with a beard!"

There was a Young Lady of Portugal,
Whose ideas were excessively nautical;
She climbed up a tree, to examine the sea,
But declared she would never leave Portugal.

There was a Young Lady of Welling,
Whose praise all the world was a telling;
She played on the harp, and caught several
    carp,
That accomplished Young Lady of Welling.

There was an Old Man of Kamschatka,
Who possessed a remarkably fat cur;
His gait and his waddle, were held as a model,
To all the fat dogs in Kamschatka.

There was an Old Man who said, "Hush!
I perceive a young bird in this bush!"
When they said—"Is it small?" he replied—"Not
    at all!
It is four times as big as the bush!"

There was a Young Lady of Tyre,
Who swept the loud chords of a lyre;
At the sound of each sweep, she enraptured the
    deep,
And enchanted the city of Tyre.

There was a Young Lady whose chin
Resembled the point of a pin;
So she had it made sharp, and purchased a
  harp,
And played several tunes with her chin.

There was an Old Man of Kilkenny,
Who never had more than a penny;
He spent all that money, in onions and honey,
That wayward Old Man of Kilkenny.

There was an Old Man with a flute,
A sarpint ran into his boot;
But he played day and night, till the sarpint
    took flight,
And avoided that Man with a flute.

There was an Old Man of the Coast,
Who placidly sat on a post;
But when it was cold, he relinquished his hold,
And called for some hot buttered toast.

There was an Old Man in a barge,
Whose nose was exceedingly large;
But in fishing by night, it supported a light,
Which helped that Old Man in a barge.

There was a Young Lady of Dorking,
Who bought a large bonnet for walking;
But its colour and size, so bedazzled her eyes,
That she very soon went back to Dorking.

There was an Old Man of the Isles,
Whose face was pervaded with smiles;
He sung high dum diddle, and played on the
    fiddle,
That amiable Man of the Isles.

There was an Old Man of the Hague,
Whose ideas were excessively vague;
He built a balloon, to examine the moon,
That deluded Old Man of the Hague.

There was a Young Lady in blue,
Who said, "Is it you? Is it you?"
When they said, "Yes, it is,"—She replied only,
  "Whizz!"
That ungracious Young Lady in blue.

There was an Old Person of Nice,
Whose associates were usually Geese;
They walked out together, in all sorts of
    weather.
That affable Person of Nice!

There was an Old Person of Tring,
Who embellished his nose with a ring;
He gazed at the moon, every evening in June,
That ecstatic Old Person of Tring.

There was an Old Person of Ealing,
Who was wholly devoid of good feeling;
He drove a small gig, with three Owls and a
     Pig,
Which distressed all the people of Ealing.

There was an Old Man of Coblenz,
The length of whose legs was immense;
He went with one prance, from Turkey to
 France,
That surprising Old Man of Coblenz.

There was a Young Lady whose bonnet
Came untied when the birds sate upon it;
But she said, "I don't care! all the birds in the
 air
Are welcome to sit on my bonnet!"

There was an Old Man of Dunrose;
A parrot seized hold of his nose;
When he grew melancholy, they said, "His
    name's Polly,"
Which soothed that Old Man of Dunrose.

There was an Old Person of Putney,
Whose food was roast spiders and chutney;
Which he took with his tea, within sight of the
    sea,
That romantic Old Person of Putney.

There was an Old Man of Three Bridges,
Whose mind was distracted by midges;
He sate on a wheel, eating underdone veal,
Which relieved that Old Man of Three Bridges.

There was an Old Man on the Border,
Who lived in the utmost disorder;
He danced with the cat, and made tea in his
    hat,
Which vexed all the folks on the Border.

There was an Old Man who said, "Well!
Will *nobody* answer this bell?
I have pulled day and night, till my hair has
grown white,
But nobody answers this bell!"

There was an Old Person of Hove,
Who frequented the depths of a grove;
Where he studied his books, with the wrens and
the rooks,
That tranquil Old Person of Hove.

There was an Old Man in a garden,
Who always begged every-one's pardon;
When they asked him, "What for?"—He replied
   "You're a bore!
And I trust you'll go out of my garden."

There was a Young Lady of Bute,
Who played on a silver-gilt flute;
She played several jigs. to her uncle's white
   pigs,
That amusing Young Lady of Bute.

There was an Old Man who supposed
That the street door was partially closed;
But some very large rats, ate his coats and his
    hats,
While that futile old gentleman dozed.

There was a Young Lady whose eyes
Were unique as to colour and size;
When she opened them wide, people all turned
    aside,
And started away in surprise.

There was an Old Man of the Wrekin,
Whose shoes made a horrible creaking;
But they said "Tell us whether, your shoes are
of leather,
Or of what, you Old Man of the Wrekin?"

There was an Old Man of the West,
Who wore a pale plum-coloured vest;
When they said, "Does it fit?" he replied, "Not a
bit!"
That uneasy Old Man of the West.

# Incidents in the Life of My Uncle Arly

### I

O My agèd Uncle Arly!
Sitting on a heap of Barley
    Thro' the silent hours of night,—
Close beside a leafy thicket:—
On his nose there was a Cricket,—
In his hat a Railway-Ticket;—
    (But his shoes were far too tight.)

### II

Long ago, in youth, he squander'd
All his goods away, and wander'd
    To the Tiniskoop-hills afar.
There on golden sunsets blazing,
Every evening found him gazing,—
Singing,—"Orb! you're quite amazing!
    "How I wonder what you are!"

### III

Like the ancient Medes and Persians,
Always by his own exertions
    He subsisted on those hills;—
Whiles,—by teaching children spelling,—
Or at times by merely yelling,—
Or at intervals by selling
    Propter's Nicodemus Pills.

**IV**

Later, in his morning rambles
He perceived the moving brambles—
    Something square and white disclose;—
'Twas a First-class Railway-Ticket;
But, on stooping down to pick it
Off the ground,—a pea-green Cricket
    Settled on my uncle's Nose.

**V**

Never—never more,—oh! never,
Did that Cricket leave him ever,—
    Dawn or evening, day or night;—
Clinging as a constant treasure,—
Chirping with a cheerious measure,—
Wholly to my uncle's pleasure,—
    (Though his shoes were far too tight.)

**VI**

So for three-and-forty winters,
Till his shoes were worn to splinters,
    All those hills he wander'd o'er,—
Sometimes silent;—sometimes yelling;—
Till he came to Borley-Melling,
Near his old ancestral dwelling;—
    (But his shoes were far too tight.)

**VII**

On a little heap of Barley
Died my agèd uncle Arly,

And they buried him one night;—
Close beside the leafy thicket;—
There,—his hat and Railway-Ticket;—
There,—his ever-faithful Cricket;—
(But his shoes were far too tight.)

## The Owl and the Pussy-cat

**I**

The Owl and the Pussy-cat went to sea
   In a beautiful pea-green boat,
They took some honey, and plenty of money,
   Wrapped up in a five-pound note.
The Owl looked up to the stars above,
   And sang to a small guitar,
"O lovely Pussy! O Pussy, my love,
   What a beautiful Pussy you are,
      You are,
      You are!
   What a beautiful Pussy you are!"

**II**

Pussy said to the Owl, "You elegant fowl!
  How charmingly sweet you sing!
O let us be married! too long we have tarried:
  But what shall we do for a ring?"
They sailed away, for a year and a day,
  To the land where the Bong-tree grows
And there in a wood a Piggy-wig stood
  With a ring at the end of his nose,
      His nose,
      His nose,
  With a ring at the end of his nose.

**III**

"Dear Pig, are you willing to sell for one shilling
  Your ring?" Said the Piggy, "I will."
So they took it away, and were married next day
  By the Turkey who lives on the hill.
They dined on mince, and slices of quince,
  Which they ate with a runcible spoon;
And hand in hand, on the edge of the sand,
  They danced by the light of the moon,
      The moon,
      The moon,
  They danced by the light of the moon.

## The Duck and the Kangaroo

**I**

Said the Duck to the Kangaroo,
  "Good gracious! how you hop!
Over the fields and the water too,
  As if you never would stop!
My life is a bore in this nasty pond,
And I long to go out in the world beyond!
  I wish I could hop like you!"
  Said the Duck to the Kangaroo.

**II**

"Please give me a ride on your back!"
  Said the Duck to the Kangaroo.
"I would sit quite still, and say nothing but
    'Quack,'
  The whole of the long day through!
And we'd go to the Dee, and the Jelly Bo Lee,

Over the land, and over the sea;—
　　Please take me a ride! O do!"
　　Said the Duck to the Kangaroo.

### III

Said the Kangaroo to the Duck,
　　"This requires some little reflection;
Perhaps on the whole it might bring me luck,
　　And there seems but one objection,
Which is, if you'll let me speak so bold,
Your feet are unpleasantly wet and cold,
　　And would probably give me the roo-
　　Matiz!" said the Kangaroo.

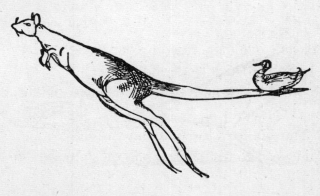

**IV**

Said the Duck, "As I sate on the rocks,
　I have thought over that completely,
And I bought four pairs of worsted socks
　Which fit my web-feet neatly.
And to keep out the cold I've bought a cloak,
And every day a cigar I'll smoke,
　All to follow my own dear true
　Love of a Kangaroo!"

**V**

Said the Kangaroo, "I'm ready!
　All in the moonlight pale;
But to balance me well, dear Duck, sit steady!
　And quite at the end of my tail!"
So away they went with a hop and a bound,
And they hopped the whole world three times
　　round;
　And who so happy,—O who,
　As the Duck and the Kangaroo?

## The Daddy Long-legs and the Fly

**I**

Once Mr. Daddy Long-legs,
  Dressed in brown and gray,
Walked about upon the sands
  Upon a summer's day;
And there among the pebbles,
  When the wind was rather cold,
He met with Mr. Floppy Fly,
  All dressed in blue and gold.
And as it was too soon to dine,
They drank some Periwinkle-wine,
And played an hour or two, or more,
At battlecock and shuttledore.

**II**

Said Mr. Daddy Long-legs
  To Mr. Floppy Fly,

"Why do you never come to court?
    I wish you'd tell me why.
All gold and shine, in dress so fine,
    You'd quite delight the court.
Why do you never go at all?
    I really think you *ought!*
And if you went, you'd see such sights!
Such rugs! and jugs! and candle-lights!
And more than all, the King and Queen,
One in red, and one in green!"

**III**

"O Mr. Daddy Long-legs,"
    Said Mr. Floppy Fly,
"It's true I never go to court,
    And I will tell you why.
If I had six long legs like yours,
    At once I'd go to court!
But oh! I can't, because *my* legs
    Are so extremely short.
And I'm afraid the King and Queen
(One in red, and one in green)
Would say aloud, 'You are not fit,
You Fly, to come to court a bit!' "

**IV**

"O Mr. Daddy Long-legs,"
    Said Mr. Floppy Fly,
"I wish you'd sing one little song!
    One mumbian melody!

You used to sing so awful well
    In former days gone by,
But now you never sing at all:
    I wish you'd tell me why:
For if you would, the silvery sound
Would please the shrimps and cockles round,
And all the crabs would gladly come
To hear you sing, 'Ah, Hum di Hum' !"

V

Said Mr. Daddy Long-legs,
    "I can never sing again!
And if you wish, I'll tell you why,
    Although it gives me pain.
For years I cannot hum a bit,
    Or sing the smallest song;
And this the dreadful reason is,
    My legs are grown too long!
My six long legs, all here and there,
Oppress my bosom with despair;
And if I stand, or lie, or sit,
I cannot sing one single bit!"

VI

So Mr. Daddy Long-legs
    And Mr. Floppy Fly
Sat down in silence by the sea,
    And gazed upon the sky.
They said, "This is a dreadful thing!
    The world has all gone wrong,

Since one has legs too short by half,
   The other much too long!
One never more can go to court,
Because his legs have grown too short;
The other cannot sing a song,
Because his legs have grown too long!"

**VII**

Then Mr. Daddy Long-legs
   And Mr. Floppy Fly
Rushed downward to the foamy sea
   With one sponge-taneous cry;
And there they found a little boat,
   Whose sails were pink and gray;
And off they sailed among the waves,
   Far, and far away.
They sailed across the silent main,
And reached the great Gromboolian plain;
And there they play for evermore
At battlecock and shuttledore.

## The Jumblies

**I**

They went to sea in a Sieve, they did,
  In a Sieve they went to sea:
In spite of all their friends could say,
On a winter's morn, on a stormy day,
  In a Sieve they went to sea!
And when the Sieve turned round and round,
And every one cried, "You'll all be drowned!"
They called aloud, "Our Sieve ain't big,
But we don't care a button! we don't care a fig!
  In a Sieve we'll go to sea!"
    Far and few, far and few,
      Are the lands where the Jumblies live;
      Their heads are green, and their hands are
        blue,
        And they went to sea in a Sieve.

**II**

They sailed away in a Sieve, they did,
   In a Sieve they sailed so fast,
With only a beautiful pea-green veil
Tied with a riband by way of a sail,
   To a small tobacco-pipe mast;
And every one said, who saw them go,
"O won't they be soon upset, you know!
For the sky is dark, and the voyage is long,
And happen what may, it's extremely wrong
   In a Sieve to sail so fast!"
      Far and few, far and few,
         Are the lands where the Jumblies live;
      Their heads are green, and their hands are
            blue,
         And they went to sea in a Sieve.

**III**

The water it soon came in, it did,
   The water it soon came in;
So to keep them dry, they wrapped their feet
In a pinky paper all folded neat,
   And they fastened it down with a pin.
And they passed the night in a crockery-jar,
And each of them said, "How wise we are!
Though the sky be dark, and the voyage be
      long,
Yet we never can think we were rash or wrong,
   While round in our Sieve we spin!"

Far and few, far and few,
    Are the lands where the Jumblies live;
Their heads are green, and their hands are
        blue,
    And they went to sea in a Sieve.

IV

And all night long they sailed away;
    And when the sun went down,
They whistled and warbled a moony song
To the echoing sound of a coppery gong,
    In the shade of the mountains brown.
"O Timballo! How happy we are,
When we live in a Sieve and a crockery-jar,
And all night long in the moonlight pale,
We sail away with a pea-green sail,
    In the shade of the mountains brown!"
        Far and few, far and few,
            Are the lands where the Jumblies live;
        Their heads are green, and their hands are
                blue,
            And they went to sea in a Sieve.

V

They sailed to the Western Sea, they did,
    To a land all covered with trees,
And they bought an Owl, and a useful Cart,
And a pound of Rice, and a Cranberry Tart,
    And a hive of silvery Bees.

And they bought a Pig, and some green
    Jack-daws,
And a lovely Monkey with lollipop paws,
And forty bottles of Ring-Bo-Ree,
    And no end of Stilton Cheese.
        Far and few, far and few,
           Are the lands where the Jumblies live;
        Their heads are green, and their hands are
           blue,
           And they went to sea in a Sieve.

**VI**

And in twenty years they all came back,
   In twenty years or more,
And every one said, "How tall they've grown!
For they've been to the Lakes, and the Torrible
    Zone,
    And the hills of the Chankly Bore."
And they drank their health, and gave them a
    feast
Of dumplings made of beautiful yeast;
And every one said, "If we only live,
We too will go to sea in a Sieve,—
    To the hills of the Chankly Bore!"
        Far and few, far and few,
           Are the lands where the Jumblies live;
        Their heads are green, and their hands are
           blue,
           And they went to sea in a Sieve.

## Calico Pie

**I**

    Calico Pie,
    The little Birds fly
Down to the calico tree,
    Their wings were blue,
    And they sang "Tilly-loo!"
    Till away they flew,—
And they never came back to me!
    They never came back!
    They never came back!
They never came back to me!

**II**

    Calico Jam,
    The little Fish swam,
Over the syllabub sea,
    He took off his hat,

To the Sole and the Sprat,
And the Willeby-wat,—
But he never came back to me!

He never came back!
He never came back!
He never came back to me!


**III**

Calico Ban,
The little Mice ran,
To be ready in time for tea,
Flippity flup,
They drank it all up,
And danced in the cup,—

But they never came back to me!
    They never came back!
    They never came back!
They never came back to me!


**IV**

    Calico Drum,
    The Grasshoppers come,
The Butterfly, Beetle, and Bee,
    Over the ground,
    Around and round,
    With a hop and a bound,—

But they never came back!
    They never came back!
    They never came back!
They never came back to me!

## The Broom, the Shovel, the Poker, and the Tongs

I

The Broom and the Shovel, the Poker and
 Tongs,
 They all took a drive in the Park,
And they each sang a song, Ding-a-dong, Ding-
 a-dong,
 Before they went back in the dark.
Mr. Poker he sate quite upright in the coach,
 Mr. Tongs made a clatter and clash,
Miss Shovel was dressed all in black (with a
 brooch),
 Mrs. Broom was in blue (with a sash).
  Ding-a-dong! Ding-a-dong!
  And they all sang a song!

**II**

"O Shovely so lovely!" the Poker he sang,
  "You have perfectly conquered my heart!
Ding-a-dong! Ding-a-dong! If you're pleased
    with my song,
  I will feed you with cold apple tart!
When you scrape up the coals with a delicate
    sound,
  You enrapture my life with delight!
Your nose is so shiny! your head is so round!
    And your shape is so slender and bright!
        Ding-a-dong! Ding-a-dong!
        Ain't you pleased with my song?"


**III**

"Alas! Mrs. Broom!" sighed the Tongs in his
    song,
  "O is it because I'm so thin,
And my legs are so long—Ding-a-dong! Ding-a-
    dong!
  That you don't care about me a pin?
Ah! fairest of creatures, when sweeping the
    room,
  Ah! why don't you heed my complaint!
Must you needs be so cruel, you beautiful
    Broom,

Because you are covered with paint?
  Ding-a-dong! Ding-a-dong!
  You are certainly wrong!"

**IV**

Mrs. Broom and Miss Shovel together they
  sang,
 "What nonsense you're singing to-day!"
Said the Shovel, "I'll certainly hit you a bang!"
 Said the Broom, "And I'll sweep you away!"
So the Coachman drove homeward as fast as he
  could,
 Perceiving their anger with pain;
But they put on the kettle, and little by little,
 They all became happy again.
  Ding-a-dong! Ding-a-dong!
  There's an end of my song!

## Mr. and Mrs. Spikky Sparrow

**I**

On a little piece of wood,
Mr. Spikky Sparrow stood;
Mrs. Sparrow sate close by,
A-making of an insect pie,
For her little children five,
In the nest and all alive,
Singing with a cheerful smile
To amuse them all the while,
  "Twikky wikky wikky wee,
  Wikky bikky twikky tee,
   Spikky bikky bee!"

**II**

Mrs. Spikky Sparrow said,
"Spikky, Darling! in my head
Many thoughts of trouble come,
Like to flies upon a plum!
All last night, among the trees,
I heard you cough, I heard you sneeze;

And, thought I, 'It's come to that
Because he does not wear a hat!'
     Chippy wippy sikky tee!
     Bikky wikky tikky mee!
      Spikky chippy wee!


**III**

"Not that you are growing old,
But the nights are growing cold.
No one stays out all night long
Without a hat: I'm sure it's wrong!"
Mr. Spikky said, "How kind,
Dear! you are, to speak your mind!
All your life I wish you luck!
You are! you are! a lovely duck!
     Witchy witchy witchy wee!
     Twitchy witchy witchy bee!
      Tikky tikky tee!


**IV**

"I was also sad, and thinking,
When one day I saw you winking,
And I heard you sniffle-snuffle,
And I saw your feathers ruffle;
To myself I sadly said,
'She's neuralgia in her head!
That dear head has nothing on it!
Ought she not to wear a bonnet?'

Witchy kitchy kitchy wee?
Spikky wikky mikky bee?
Chippy wippy chee?

## V

"Let us both fly up to town!
There I'll buy you such a gown!
Which, completely in the fashion,
You shall tie a sky-blue sash on.
And a pair of slippers neat,
To fit your darling little feet,
So that you will look and feel
Quite galloobious and genteel!
Jikky wikky bikky see,
Chicky bikky wikky bee,
Twicky witchy wee!"

## VI

So they both to London went,
Alighting on the Monument,
Whence they flew down swiftly—pop,
Into Moses' wholesale shop;
There they bought a hat and bonnet,
And a gown with spots upon it,
A satin sash of Cloxam blue,
And a pair of slippers too.
Zikky wikky mikky bee,
Witchy witchy mitchy kee,
Sikky tikky wee.

**VII**

Then when so completely drest,
Back they flew, and reached their nest.
Their children cried, "O Ma and Pa!
How truly beautiful you are!"
Said they, "We trust that cold or pain
We shall never feel again!
While, perched on tree, or house, or steeple,
We now shall look like other people.

    Witchy witchy witchy wee,
     Twikky mikky bikky bee,
      Zikky sikky tee."

## The Table and the Chair

I

Said the Table to the Chair,
"You can hardly be aware,
How I suffer from the heat,
And from chilblains on my feet!
If we took a little walk,
We might have a little talk!
Pray let us take the air!"
Said the Table to the Chair.

II

Said the Chair unto the Table,
"Now you *know* we are not able!
How foolishly you talk,
When you know we *cannot* walk!"
Said the Table, with a sigh,
"It can do no harm to try,
I've as many legs as you,
Why can't we walk on two?"

**III**

So they both went slowly down,
And walked about the town
With a cheerful bumpy sound,
As they toddled round and round.
And everybody cried,
As they hastened to their side,
"See! the Table and the Chair
Have come out to take the air!"

**IV**

But in going down an alley,
To a castle in a valley,
They completely lost their way,
And wandered all the day,

Till, to see them safely back,
They paid a Ducky-quack,
And a Beetle, and a Mouse,
Who took them to their house.

V

Then they whispered to each other,
"O delightful little brother!
What a lovely walk we've taken!
Let us dine on Beans and Bacon!"
So the Ducky, and the leetle
Browny-Mousy and the Beetle
Dined, and danced upon their heads
Till they toddled to their beds.

## The Courtship of the Yonghy-Bonghy-Bò

I

On the Coast of Coromandel
Where the early pumpkins blow,
In the middle of the woods
   Lived the Yonghy-Bonghy-Bò.
Two old chairs, and half a candle,—
One old jug without a handle,—
     These were all his worldly goods:
     In the middle of the woods,
     These were all the worldly goods,
   Of the Yonghy-Bonghy-Bò,
   Of the Yonghy-Bonghy-Bò.

**II**

Once, among the Bong-trees walking
  Where the early pumpkins blow,
    To a little heap of stones
    Came the Yonghy-Bonghy-Bò.
There he heard a Lady talking,
To some milk-white Hens of Dorking,—
    " 'Tis the Lady Jingly Jones!
    On that little heap of stones
    Sits the Lady Jingly Jones'."
  Said the Yonghy-Bonghy-Bò,
  Said the Yonghy-Bonghy-Bò.

**III**

"Lady Jingly! Lady Jingly!
  Sitting where the pumpkins blow,
    Will you come and be my wife?"
  Said the Yonghy-Bonghy-Bò.
"I am tired of living singly,—
On this coast so wild and shingly,—
    I'm a-weary of my life:
    If you'll come and be my wife,
    Quite serene would be my life!"—
  Said the Yonghy-Bonghy-Bò,
  Said the Yonghy-Bonghy-Bò.

**IV**

"On this Coast of Coromandel,
  Shrimps and watercresses grow,
    Prawns are plentiful and cheap,"

Said the Yonghy-Bonghy-Bò.
"You shall have my Chairs and candle,
And my jug without a handle!—
    Gaze upon the rolling deep
    (Fish is plentiful and cheap)
    As the sea, my love is deep!"
  Said the Yonghy-Bonghy-Bò,
  Said the Yonghy-Bonghy-Bò.

V

Lady Jingly answered sadly,
  And her tears began to flow,—
    "Your proposal comes too late,
    Mr. Yonghy-Bonghy-Bò!
I would be your wife most gladly!"
(Here she twirled her fingers madly,)
    "But in England I've a mate!
    Yes! you've asked me far too late,
    For in England I've a mate,
    Mr. Yonghy-Bonghy-Bò!
    Mr. Yonghy-Bonghy-Bò!"

VI

"Mr. Jones—(his name is Handel,—
  Handel Jones, Esquire, & Co.)
    Dorking fowls delights to send,
    Mr. Yonghy-Bonghy-Bò!
Keep, oh! keep your Chairs and candle,
And your jug without a handle,—
    I can merely be your friend!

—Should my Jones more Dorkings send,
　　I will give you three, my friend!
Mr. Yonghy-Bonghy-Bò!
Mr. Yonghy-Bonghy-Bò!"

**VII**

"Though you've such a tiny body,
　　And your head so large doth grow,—
　　　Though your hat may blow away,
　　Mr. Yonghy-Bonghy-Bò!
Though you're such a Hoddy Doddy—
Yet I wish that I could modi-
　　　fy the words I needs must say!
　　　Will you please to go away?
　　　That is all I have to say—
　　Mr. Yonghy-Bonghy-Bò!
　　Mr. Yonghy-Bonghy-Bò!"

**VIII**

Down the slippery slopes of Myrtle,
　　Where the early pumpkins blow.
　　　To the calm and silent sea
　　Fled the Yonghy-Bonghy-Bò.
There, beyond the Bay of Gurtle,
Lay a large and lively Turtle;—
　　　"You're the Cove," he said, "for me
　　　On your back beyond the sea.
　　　Turtle, you shall carry me!"
　　Said the Yonghy-Bonghy-Bò,
　　Said the Yonghy-Bonghy-Bò.

**IX**

Through the silent-roaring ocean
    Did the Turtle swiftly go;
        Holding fast upon his shell
    Rode the Yonghy-Bonghy-Bò.
With a sad primæval motion
Towards the sunset isles of Boshen
        Still the Turtle bore him well.
        Holding fast upon his shell,
        "Lady Jingly Jones, farewell!"
    Sang the Yonghy-Bonghy-Bò,
    Sang the Yonghy-Bonghy-Bò.


**X**

From the Coast of Coromandel,
    Did that Lady never go;
        On that heap of stones she mourns
    For the Yonghy-Bonghy-Bò.

On that Coast of Coromandel,
In his jug without a handle
    Still she weeps, and daily moans;
    On that little heap of stones
    To her Dorking Hens she moans,
  For the Yonghy-Bonghy-Bò,
  For the Yonghy-Bonghy-Bò.

## The Nutcrackers and the Sugar-tongs

**I**

The Nutcrackers sate by a plate on the table,
  The Sugar-tongs sate by a plate at his side;
And the Nutcrackers said, "Don't you wish we
    were able
  Along the blue hills and green meadows to
    ride?
Must we drag on this stupid existence for ever,
  So idle and weary, so full of remorse,—
While every one else takes his pleasure, and
    never
  Seems happy unless he is riding a horse?"

**II**

"Don't you think we could ride without being
    instructed?
  Without any saddle, or bridle, or spur?
Our legs are so long, and so aptly constructed,
  I'm sure that an accident could not occur.

Let us all of a sudden hop down from the table,
  And hustle downstairs, and each jump on a
    horse!
Shall we try? Shall we go? Do you think we are
    able?"
  The Sugar-tongs answered distinctly, "Of
    course!"

**III**

So down the long staircase they hopped in a
    minute,
  The Sugar-tongs snapped, and the Crackers
    said "crack!"
The stable was open, the horses were in it;
  Each took out a pony, and jumped on his
    back.
The Cat in a fright scrambled out of the door-
    way,
  The Mice tumbled out of a bundle of hay,
The brown and white Rats, and the black ones
    from Norway,
  Screamed out, "They are taking the horses
    away!"

**IV**

The whole of the household was filled with
    amazement,

The Cups and the Saucers danced madly
about,
The Plates and the Dishes looked out of the
casement,
The Saltcellar stood on his head with a shout,
The Spoons with a clatter looked out of the
lattice,
The Mustard-pot climbed up the Gooseberry
Pies,
The Soup-ladle peeped through a heap of Veal
Patties,
And squeaked with a ladle-like scream of sur-
prise.

V

The Frying-pan said, "It's an awful delusion!"
The Tea-kettle hissed and grew black in the
face;
And they all rushed downstairs in the wildest
confusion,
To see the great Nutcracker-Sugar-tong race.
And out of the stable, with screamings and
laughter,
(Their ponies were cream-coloured, speckled
with brown,)
The Nutcrackers first, and the Sugar-tongs
after,

Rode all round the yard, and then all round
the town.

**VI**

They rode through the street, and they rode by
the station,
They galloped away to the beautiful shore;
In silence they rode, and "made no observa-
tion,"
Save this: "We will never go back any more!"
And still you might hear, till they rode out of
hearing,
The Sugar-tongs snap, and the Crackers say
"crack!"
Till far in the distance their forms disappearing,
They faded away.—And they never came back!

## The Quangle Wangle's Hat

I

On the top of the Crumpetty Tree
    The Quangle Wangle sat,
But his face you could not see,
    On account of his Beaver Hat.
For his Hat was a hundred and two feet wide,
With ribbons and bibbons on every side
And bells, and buttons, and loops, and lace,
So that nobody ever could see the face
            Of the Quangle Wangle Quee.

II

The Quangle Wangle said
    To himself on the Crumpetty Tree,—
"Jam; and jelly; and bread;
    Are the best food for me!

But the longer I live on this Crumpetty Tree
The plainer than ever it seems to me
That very few people come this way
And that life on the whole is far from gay!"
      Said the Quangle Wangle Quee.

**III**

But there came to the Crumpetty Tree,
   Mr. and Mrs. Canary;
And they said,—"Did you ever see
   Any spot so charmingly airy?
May we build a nest on your lovely Hat?
Mr. Quangle Wangle, grant us that!
O please let us come and build a nest
Of whatever material suits you best,
      Mr. Quangle Wangle Quee!"

**IV**

And besides, to the Crumpetty Tree
   Came the Stork, the Duck, and the Owl;
The Snail, and the Bumble-Bee,
   The Frog, and the Fimble Fowl;
(The Fimble Fowl, with a Corkscrew leg;)
And all of them said,—"We humbly beg,
We may build our homes on your lovely Hat,—
Mr. Quangle Wangle, grant us that!
      Mr. Quangle Wangle Quee!"

**V**

And the Golden Grouse came there,
   And the Pobble who has no toes,—

And the small Olympian bear,—
  And the Dong with a luminous nose.
And the Blue Baboon, who played the flute,—
And the Orient Calf from the Land of Tute,—
And the Attery Squash, and the Bisky Bat,—
All came and built on the lovely Hat
     Of the Quangle Wangle Quee.

**VI**

And the Quangle Wangle said
  To himself on the Crumpetty Tree,—
"When all these creatures move
  What a wonderful noise there'll be!"
And at night by the light of the Mulberry moon
They danced to the Flute of the Blue Baboon,
On the broad green leaves of the Crumpetty
    Tree,
And all were as happy as happy could be,
     With the Quangle Wangle Quee.